Telling the Truth

Story by Dawn McMillan
Illustrations by Vasja Koman

Rigby®
A Harcourt Achieve Imprint

www.Rigby.com
1-800-531-5015

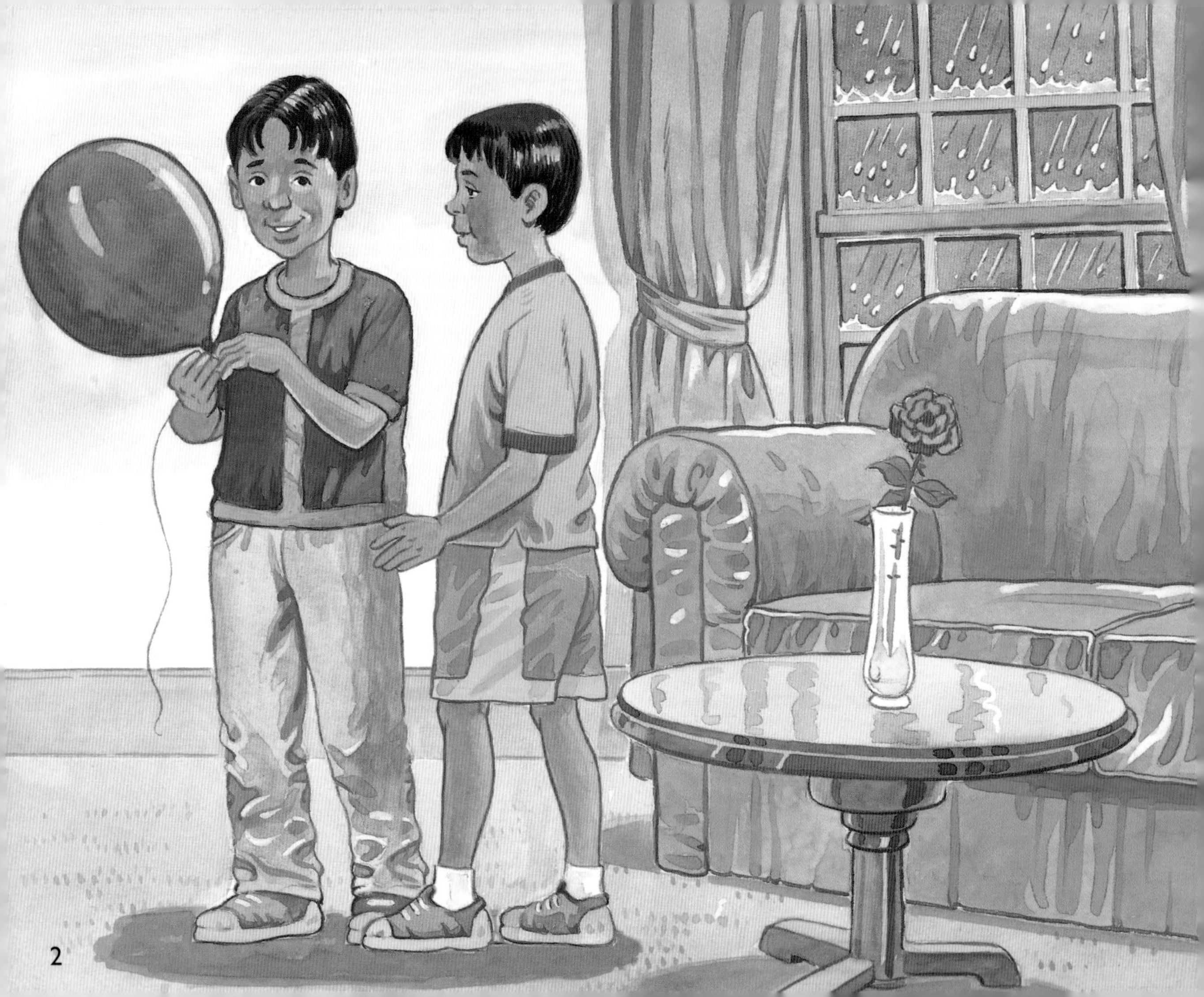

It was a rainy day, so Rico and Jorge had to play inside.

"Let's play with this balloon, Rico," said Jorge.
"I will hit it around the room, and you can try to catch it!"

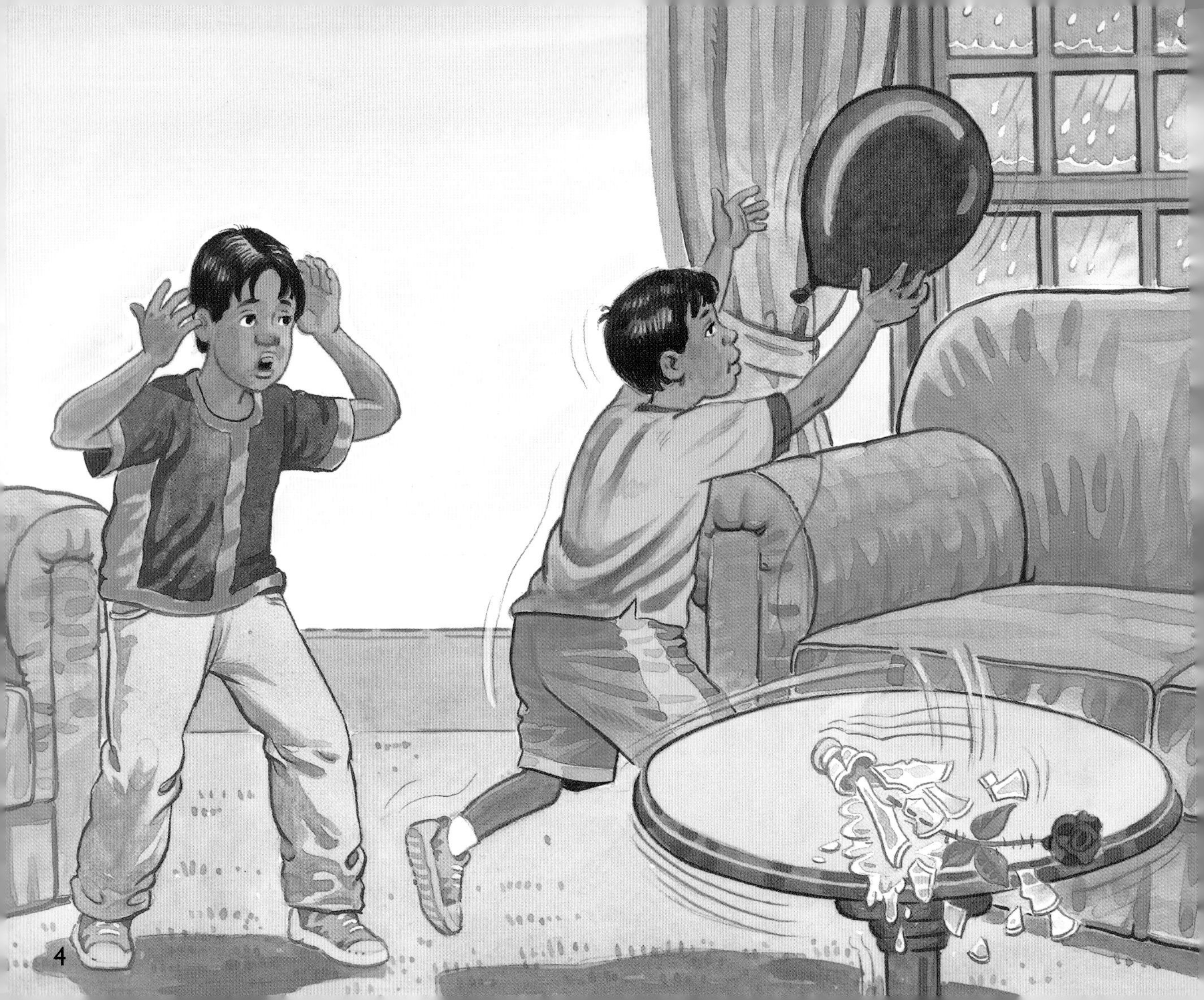

Rico jumped up to catch the balloon.

He bumped the table,

and the vase fell over.

Crash!

"Oh no!" said Jorge.

"We have broken Mom's vase!"

Mom came into the room.

"Oh dear!" she said.

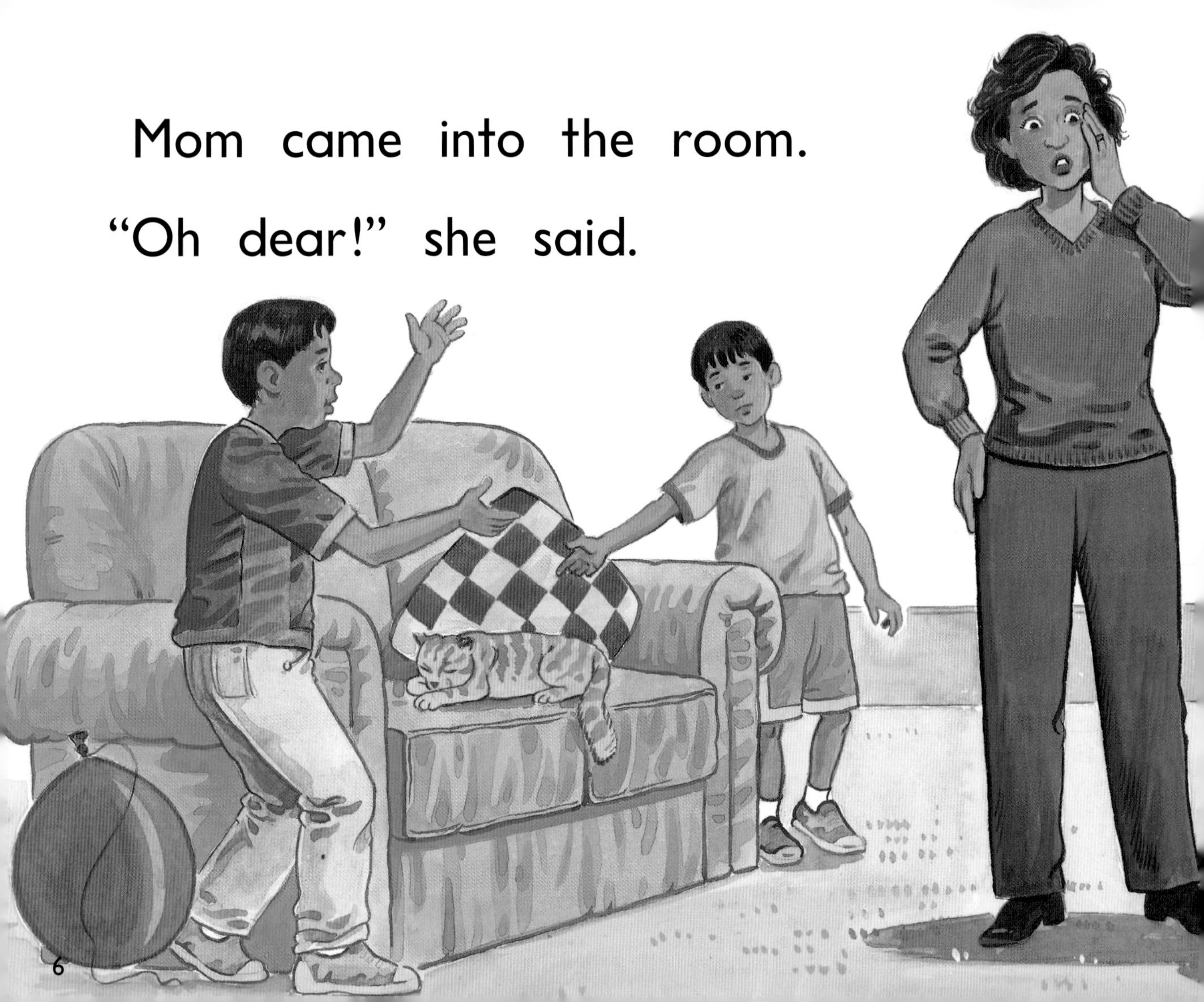

"The cat did it, Mom," said Rico.

"Yes," said Jorge,

"Tiger jumped up on the table,

and your vase fell over."

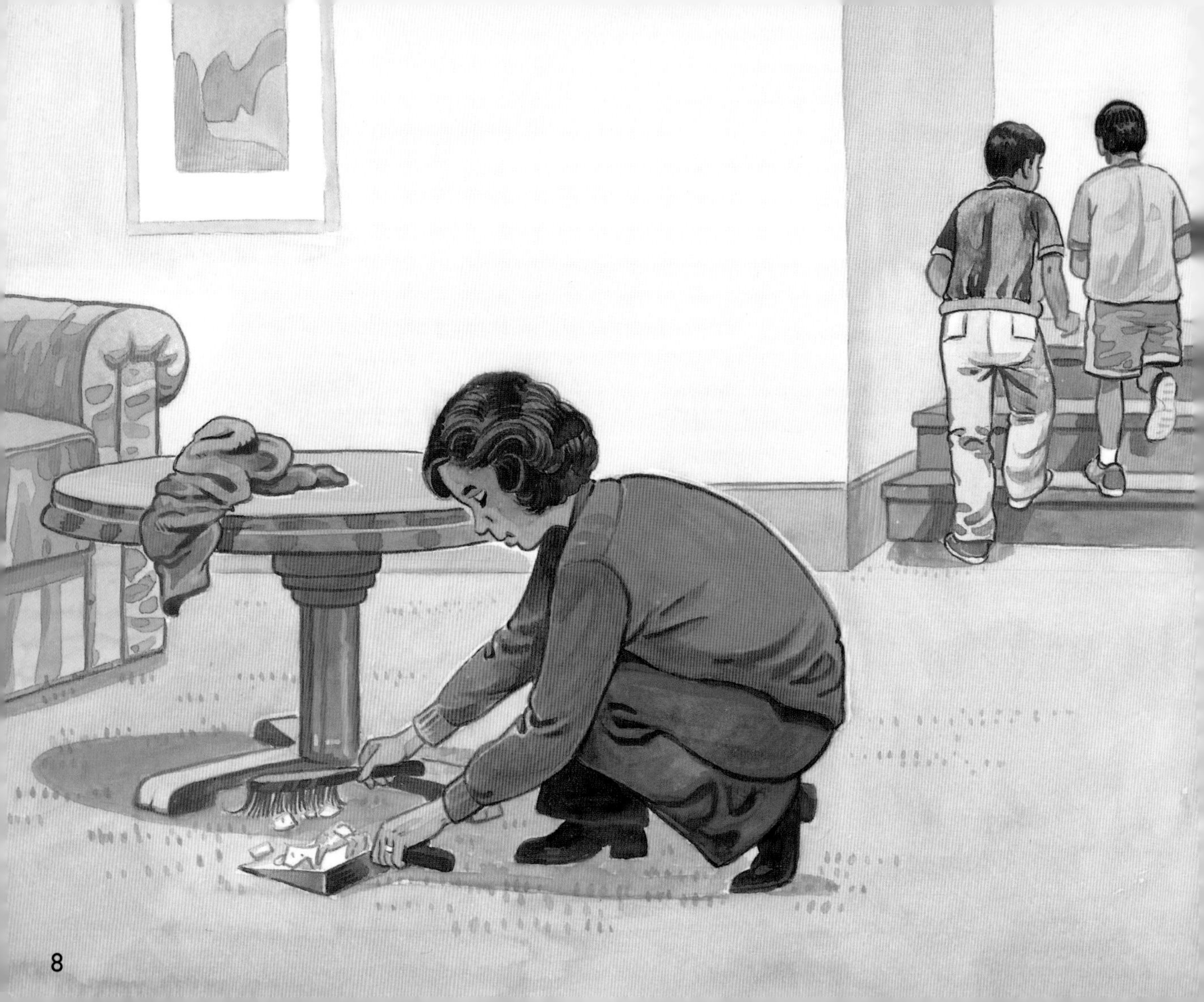

Mom cleaned up the broken vase, and Jorge and Rico went upstairs to their room.

"We didn't tell Mom the truth," said Jorge.

"I don't feel very well," said Rico.

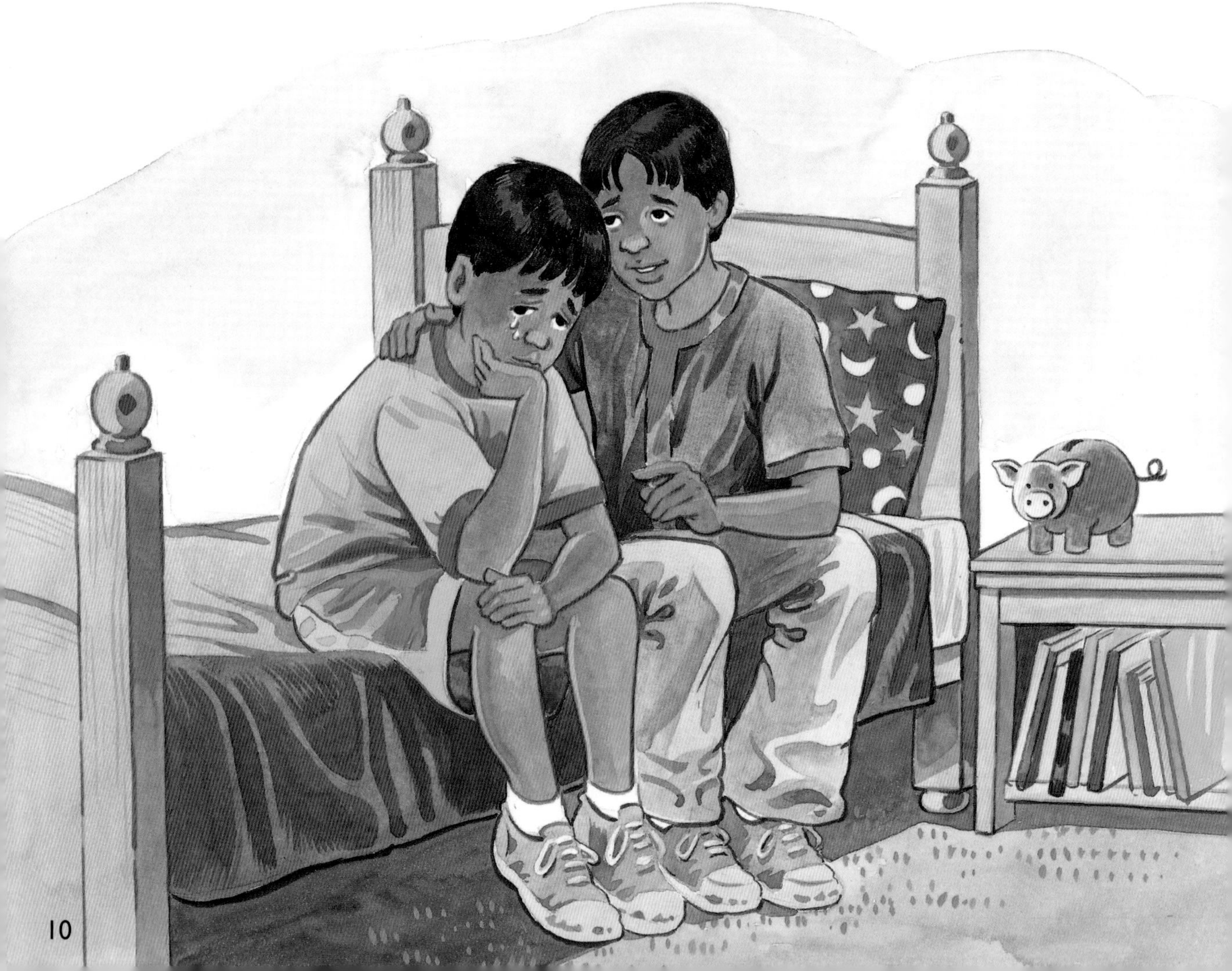

Rico started to cry.

Jorge put his arm around Rico.
"We can buy Mom a new vase,"
he said.
"We have money in our piggy banks.
But right now we have to go
and tell her the truth."

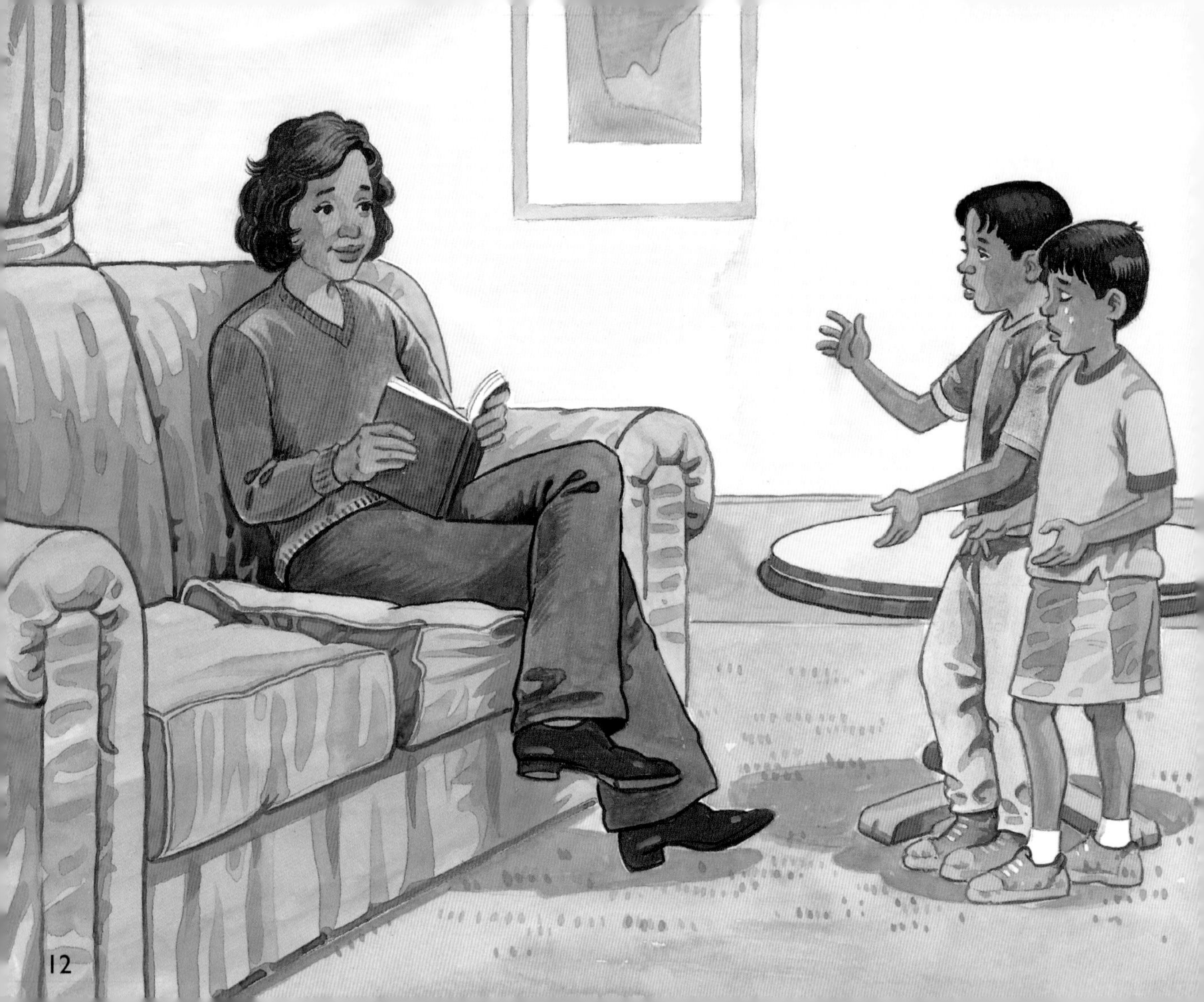

The boys went downstairs.

"Mom," said Jorge, "Tiger was asleep. He didn't make your vase fall over."

"It was us, Mom," said Rico. "We were playing with the balloon, and we bumped the table. We are **very** sorry!"

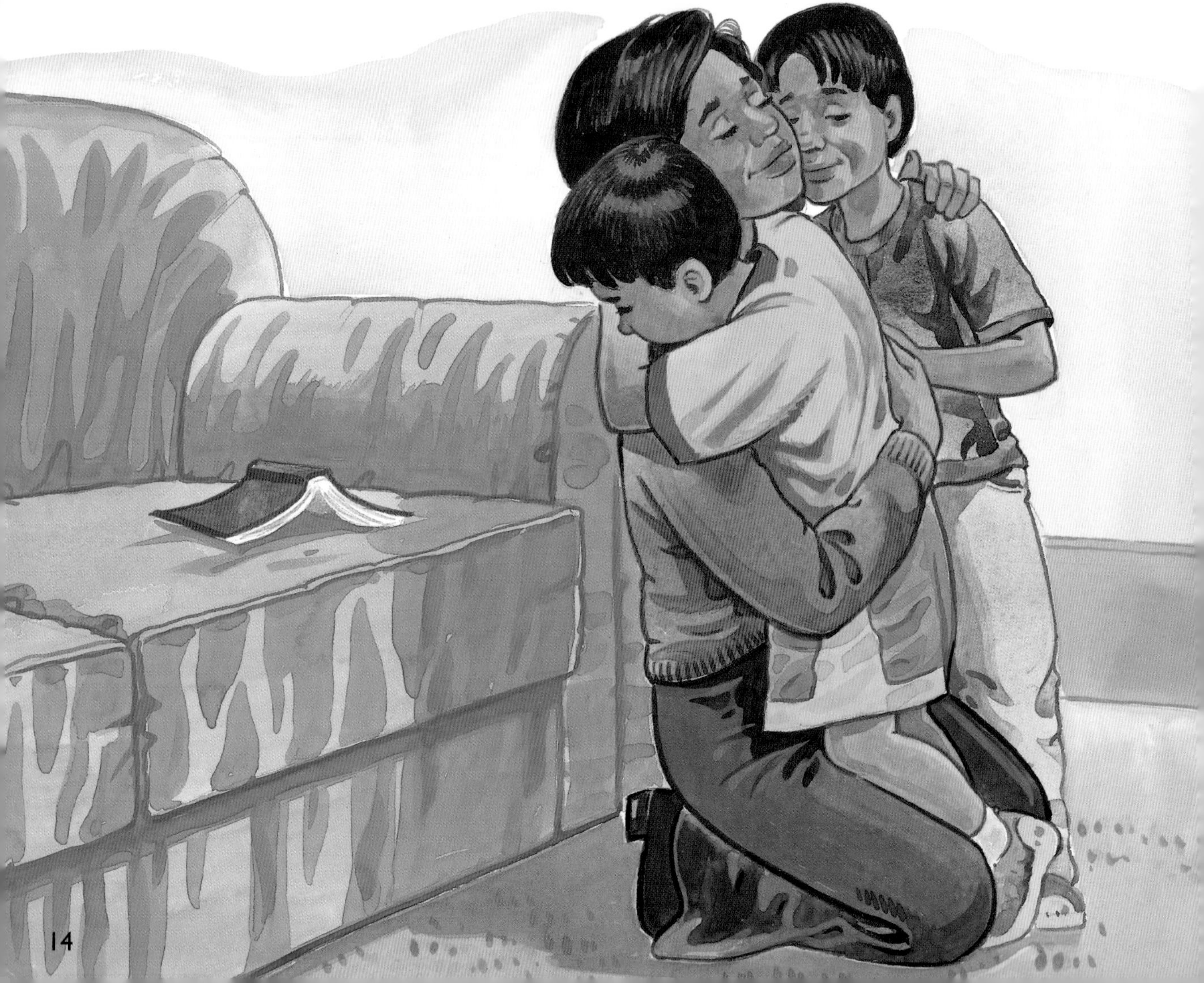

"Thank you, boys," said Mom
as she hugged them.
"I'm so pleased that you came
to tell me the truth."

"I'm pleased, too," said Jorge.

"Oh!" smiled Rico.

"I feel better now!"

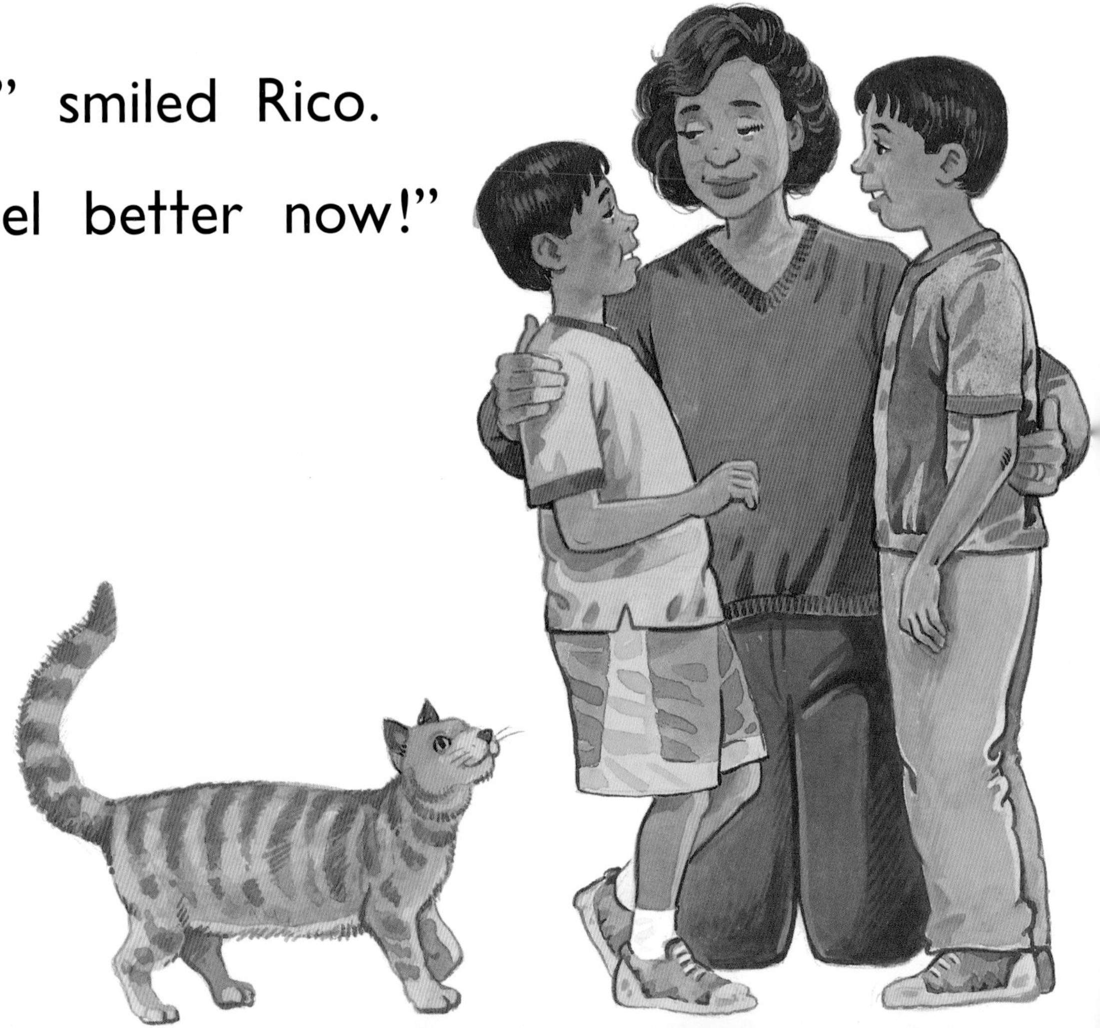